AF446633

A RECKONING
AT
CALDWELL RANCH

DENNIS H. WILLIAMS

THE WILD
BUNCH
20 FILM 24
FESTIVAL
Best Arizona Modern Western
Manuscript - "A Reckoning
at Caldwell Ranch"
by Dennis H. Williams

Author's Note:

I dedicate this and all my books to my dear mother, Eva Lee Williams.

The cover art was drawn by her.

Chapter 1

The acrid smell of diesel filled the air as the big grey dog bus rumbled into the dusty terminal, its engine a throaty growl that echoed through the summer heat. The afternoon sun cast long shadows on the cracked pavement, highlighting the worn lines and faded paint of the station. As the bus came to a halt, the screech of the air brakes pierced the otherwise quiet scene, sending a few nearby birds fluttering away in alarm. The door swung open with a hiss, and the hot, dry air rushed into the cool interior, mingling with the scent of vinyl seats and the faint, lingering aroma of stale coffee from the onboard machine.

The driver, a stout man with a weathered face, skipped down the steps, adjusting his uniform jacket as he moved. The fabric of his jacket rustled softly, contrasting with the metallic clank of the cargo hatch being unlocked. As he lifted the heavy lid, the compartment's interior was bathed in the harsh sunlight, revealing suitcases and duffel bags stacked haphazardly.

The passengers began to disembark, their footsteps heavy and deliberate, the soles of their shoes scraping against the gritty concrete. The driver handed out the luggage with practiced efficiency, his fingers brushing against the warm, sunbaked surfaces of the bags. The air was thick with the smell of sweat and the faint, sweet scent of blooming creosote bushes carried by a gentle breeze.

The fifth passenger was a dark-complected man with dark, almost black hair that cascaded just enough to touch the collar of his well-worn cotton Wrangler shirt. His black Resistol hat, slightly dusty from the journey, covered his hair and cast a shadow over his chiseled face, which remained hidden behind a pair of mirrored aviator sunglasses. The harsh sunlight reflected off his lenses, momentarily blinding anyone who glanced his way. He carried his only luggage, a weathered, soft-sided carry-on bag that swung slightly with each step.

The air around him was thick with the lingering smell of diesel and the faint scent of the creosote bushes that lined the station's outskirts. He looked neither right nor left, his stride purposeful and steady as he headed towards the back door of the terminal. The rubber soles of his boots made a soft, rhythmic thud against the cracked pavement, a sound almost drowned out by the distant hum of cicadas.

Stepping inside, he moved to the side, careful not to block the door as other passengers streamed in behind him. The sudden shift from the blinding Arizona sun to the dim, artificial lighting of the terminal caused him to pause, allowing his eyes to adjust. The cool air inside was a stark contrast to the sweltering heat outside, carrying the faint smell of industrial cleaner and a hint of stale popcorn from the nearby snack counter. He scanned the lobby, his gaze sweeping over the worn leather benches and faded posters on the walls, but he didn't see what he was looking for. The low murmur of conversations and the occasional crackle of the PA system announcing arrivals and departures filled the air, creating a backdrop of muted noise that seemed to cocoon him in a bubble of anonymity.

A voice behind him said, "Go out the front door, turn left, and get in the green Chevy pickup. I'll be there in a moment."

The dark man walked across the lobby with a quiet confidence, his boots making muted clicks against the tiled floor. The smell of the terminal, a mix of sweat, old coffee, and cleaning solution, faded as he pushed through the glass door and stepped back into the sweltering afternoon heat. He squinted against the glare of the sun, making his way to the green Chevy parked in the shade of a scraggly mesquite tree. The truck's paint was faded and chipped, a testament to many years under the relentless Arizona sun.

He dropped his bag in the back as he slid into the passenger seat, the old leather creaking under his weight. The interior of the truck was hot, the air thick with the scent of cracked vinyl, sunbaked upholstery, and the faint hint of gasoline. A second later, Julian Ralston, a tall man with a rugged demeanor, got behind the wheel. His face was lined from years of hard work, and his hands bore the calluses of a life spent outdoors. Without a word, he turned the key, and the engine roared to life, the sound of a low rumble that vibrated through the seats.

Julian dropped the truck into gear and eased it out of the parking lot, merging smoothly into the sparse afternoon traffic. The old Chevy rattled slightly, its suspension creaking with each bump in the road. As they drove through the south-central Arizona farming community, the scent of freshly turned earth and ripening crops wafted through the open windows, mingling with the dry, dusty air. The fields stretched out on either side, green and gold patches under the relentless sun, with irrigation ditches glistening in the light.

The truck headed south, the tires crunching on the gravel road and throwing up a dust cloud that billowed behind them like a ghostly trail. The landscape gradually shifted from cultivated fields to more rugged, arid terrain, dotted with cacti and scrub brush. The only sounds inside the truck were the hum of the engine, the rhythmic thump of the tires on the uneven road, and the occasional sigh of wind through the open windows. Not a word was uttered, both men lost in their own thoughts as the miles slipped by, the silence heavy but not uncomfortable.

Julian broke the silence with a sideways glance, his eyes briefly meeting Vince's, "Good to see you back, Vince."

The man half-smiled and met the sideways look, "Thanks, good to be back. But what's with the cloak and dagger stuff, and where is Kate?" Vince Caldwell asked as the truck bounced through a couple of potholes, the jarring motion making him grip the door handle, "Hey, you trying to bounce me out already?"

Julian laughed, a short, rough sound that quickly faded. The landscape outside was a blur of dusty roads and sprawling desert, the sun casting long shadows as it dipped lower in the sky. Julian's laughter died away, replaced by a somber tone as he responded, "When Pat and his buddies found out your case had been overturned and you were coming back, they got scared, real scared. We tried to keep it quiet around town when you would be getting in." The truck's engine hummed steadily, the rhythmic sound of gravel crunching under the tires accompanying his words.

Vince could see the tension in Julian's knuckles, white against the steering wheel. The cab of the truck seemed to grow hotter, the air stifling despite the breeze from the open windows. "Knowing Pat and them, I wouldn't be surprised if they didn't try to kill you. He's done it before, ya know?" Julian's voice trembled slightly, the fear evident.

The words hung heavy in the air, mixing with the dusty smell of the desert and the faint scent of sagebrush. Vince's half-smile faded, replaced by a look of grim determination. The sun continued its descent, casting an orange glow over the rugged terrain, the light flickering through the truck's windows as they drove. Vince turned his gaze back to the road ahead, the weight of Julian's words settling over him like a shroud.

"Where is Kate, Julian?" Vince insisted, his voice edged with a mix of worry and frustration.

Julian looked straight ahead, the lines of tension on his face deepening. He took a long moment to reply, the silence stretching uncomfortably between them. When he finally spoke, his eyes remained fixed on the road. "We don't know."

Vince started to speak, a sharp retort forming on his lips, but a jarring pothole bounced the words out of him, leaving him momentarily speechless. Julian continued, his voice steady but low, the weight of the situation evident. "She disappeared four days ago. She left you a note at your place. We didn't read it. We were able to save the house and corrals from the bank, but Pat must have an in at the state land department. He got your state leases. I got your truck, trailer, and your horses and gear at my place. Kate has been waiting tables at the Cash Box Cafe. I usually saw her once or twice a day, but four days ago she didn't come by. We've been looking ever since."

Julian's voice dropped to almost a whisper, the fear and concern clear. Vince's heart pounded in his chest, a mix of anger and dread tightening his throat. "What about my cattle? Did Pat get them too?" Vince growled, his hands clenching into fists.

"As far as anybody knows, the cattle are still there. But Pat turned 800 steers in with them. We figure he will gather all of them together and ship them. He still has that crooked brand inspector coming around," Julian explained, his voice tinged with helpless frustration.

"I'll get the cattle gathered before then. I'm more concerned about Kate. You got no idea where she went?"

Vince pleaded, his voice breaking slightly, the desperation clear.

The truck hit another bump, but this time Vince barely noticed. The landscape outside blurred as his thoughts raced, the dry desert air filling his lungs with each shallow breath. Julian shook his head slightly, the movement almost imperceptible. "No idea, Vince. We've searched everywhere we could think of. It's like she just vanished."

Vince Caldwell had just been released from prison. Pat Borrego had engineered a phony cattle theft case to get him convicted and sentenced to a six-year term in the state prison. His girlfriend, Kate Moreno, was to keep watch on his outfit while his friends, headed up by Julian, had hired a competent attorney and worked to get the case to a higher court where it was overturned. But Vince had still been locked up for five months. Everything Vince had ever worked for was in that little ranch, but Pat Borrego ran the county. He owned the judge, the prosecuting attorney, and the brand inspector. The worst part of the evidence that was used against him came from the brand inspector. It was an audio tape that had been altered. The owner of the cattle Vince was supposed to have stolen was a gunsel who Pat had intimidated into accusing Vince of the theft.

At Vince's house, he got out and went inside and returned with the letter Kate had left. He read it as he came back to Julian's truck. Looking up to Julian, he said, "She said Pacer, that scar-faced foreman of Pat's, came to the Cash Box and told her he was coming to take her out. She was leaving as soon as she got home. She would call you and tell you where she was."

"She has never called, Vince, I swear!" Julian shook his head.

Weeds had grown up in the horse corrals and the barn was empty of the hay Vince had stored there. Tire tracks went through the corrals and into the ranch. The gates stood open.

"Are these 40 acres still mine?" Vince asked.

"Yes, sir. The bank was threatening foreclosure, but me and the boys scratched up the money to keep the payments made. Damn Pat owns that banker too. But I think he knows he better follow the rules. Too many of us know the story. Let's go home, Margie will have a welcome home dinner for you. Then we can make a plan on getting your cattle and finding Kate," Julian started the truck.

Chapter 2

As Julian wheeled the Chevy truck into his yard, Vince could see a dozen cars and trucks parked haphazardly around the dusty expanse. The late afternoon sun cast long shadows over the vehicles, the metal glinting in the golden light. The smell of warm engine oil and the faint scent of sagebrush filled the air, mingling with the distant aroma of grilling meat. Vince turned a wary eye to Ralston, who just ducked his head and grinned.

"Welcoming home party, Vince. Margie pulled it together," Julian explained, his voice carrying a note of pride.

On Julian's front porch sat a handful of men in big hats, boots, and denim britches. The porch boards creaked under their weight as they shifted, each man etched in the deep lines of sun and hard work. Some smoked cigarettes, their acrid scent blending with the sweeter, richer aroma of cigars and pipes. Most had a can of beer in hand, the metal cold and damp with condensation, while others cradled glasses of amber-colored whiskey, the sharp, smoky scent of the alcohol hanging in the warm air.

As Vince walked up, they all stood and tried to talk at once, a cacophony of welcoming voices. Vince just nodded and shook hands with each and every one, feeling the rough calluses of their palms, the silent testament to their shared life of labor. These were the honest folks of the community, small, hardworking farmers and ranchers who lived in a worry-filled world but faced it with quiet resilience.

Inside, the house was filled with the savory smells of home-cooked food: simmering stew, freshly baked bread, and roasting meat. Margie, a robust woman with a heart as big as the sky, dropped her spoon in a pot on the stove and ran to Vince, throwing her arms around him and hugging him so tight he couldn't breathe. Tears ran down her face, leaving tracks through the flour dusted on her cheeks. The room filled with applause as everyone stood, their faces beaming with genuine joy.

Vince looked around, then at Margie, his eyes misting slightly. "You got somethin' to eat? I'm starved."

Margie disengaged and turned to the kitchen, her voice bright with emotion. "It's all ready, you all get a plate."

Vince was pushed to the front of the line, the others stepping aside with pats on the back and murmurs of encouragement. He filled his plate high with food, the smells tantalizing and comforting. He fished in a wash tub filled with ice, beer, and other drinks, the cold biting his fingers as he grabbed a beer. Taking his plate, he moved back outside and sat on the porch steps to eat, the wood warm under him from the day's sun.

"First decent meal I've had in 5 months," he said to no one in particular, his voice carrying a hint of melancholy and relief.

Everyone was silent as they ate, the only sounds were the occasional murmur of conversation and the clink of cutlery against plates. Vince kept looking around, his eyes scanning the crowd as if searching for someone. Of all the people here, Kate was the one he wanted to see most. The absence gnawed at him, a void amid the celebration.

When he had finished eating, Vince carried his plate back inside to the wreck pan, the soapy water swirling with bits of food and grease. As he turned, he came face to face with Hi Green, a local farmer. Hi's weathered face broke into a warm, welcoming smile, the scent of hay and earth clinging to his clothes.

"Good to have you back, Vince," Hi said, his voice gruff but kind, a hand extended in greeting. "What you going to do about Pat?" The two exchanged a quick firm shake.

"I'm gonna gather my cattle, find Kate, and let the lawyers figure it out. I don't want no trouble. I think Pat will get his comeuppance soon enough without my help," Vince stared at Hi.

"But he did you wrong. Ain't you gonna get even? You can do it, can't you?" Hi almost squeaked as he talked.

"No, I'm not going after him. I just couldn't understand why me?" Vince was shaking his head.

"You don't know? Why, your ranch is the best route into town with the drugs he brings up from Mexico. With you gone, he has a broadway all the way up the line." Hi couldn't talk fast enough.

"Well, that makes sense. But the law needs to handle him. I left all that get even stuff in 'Nam. I just want a quiet life. When Kate shows up, we are going to be the most boring couple you ever saw!" Vince smiled at Hi. Vince stepped around Hi and pulled another beer from the tub.

Julian Walked over to Hi, "don't look so shocked. I know Vince was a ring-tailed terror in Vietnam. We all know he could finish off Pat Borrego," his voice low so it didn't carry, "Since he met Kate, Vince hasn't been that guy."

"He got me once, Hi." Vince returned with the retrieved beer in hand. He took a drink and continued, "I believed everyone would see through the scam. But it cost all you, my friends, money and time helping me. I appreciate it and I'll make a point of paying you all back. But snuffing Pat? No, for sure I'd go to prison again for good. Our attorney is talking to the state attorney general. Let's give them a chance." Vince saluted with his beer as he went out the door.

Chapter 3

A few days later, Vince was at the feed store, his truck backed up to the loading dock where the warehouse workers were throwing a couple of sacks of grain in the back. The air was thick with the earthy scent of feed and the tang of motor oil, mingling with the warm, dusty smell of the gravel parking lot. As Vince walked through the store to pay for the grain, the creaking wooden floorboards beneath his boots added a rhythm to his steps. The store was filled with the low hum of a ceiling fan and the occasional clinking of metal tools.

He noticed a short line of three people ahead of him at the cashier's counter. The head of the line was a tall, gangly man in a dirty denim shirt, his posture slouched and weary. As he accepted his change, he turned slightly, revealing a large white bandage taped to his face from below his eye to just above his chin, covering the side of his face. The bandage was stark against his tanned skin, a glaring reminder of some recent injury.

A gasp escaped the woman directly behind the scarecrow of a man, her hand flying to her mouth. The man's eyes, already darting nervously, widened in terror when he saw Vince standing there in line. His face paled, and without a word, he rushed to the double doors, shoving them open so forcefully that they knocked down a man trying to come in. The commotion drew the attention of everyone in the store, the sudden noise jarring against the otherwise mundane afternoon.

The stayed open and Vince watched as the man sprinted to his truck, the engine roaring to life with a thunderous growl. The vehicle sped out of the gravel parking lot, spraying rocks and dust in all directions, the sound of tires skidding and gravel crunching filling the air. "What ya think got into that guy?" Vince asked no one in particular, his brow furrowed in confusion.

As Vince finished paying for his grain he turned to leave, facing the doorway. A glance through the still-open doors revealed that a deputy's vehicle had driven up next to his truck, the sound of the car's engine settling into a low idle. The deputy, a burly man with a no-nonsense demeanor softened by a hint of concern, stepped out and walked up to Vince as he was exiting, gravel from the parking lot crunching under his boots.

"I need you to come with me, Vince. You can park your truck over there; it will be safe here," the deputy said, his voice steady but carrying an undercurrent of urgency.

"Just what did I do now?" Vince demanded, a mix of irritation and worry flashing across his face.

"Nothing. I just need you to come along. You're not under arrest. It's important, though," the deputy seemed apologetic, his eyes sincere and almost pleading.

The feed store's familiar smells of grain, leather, and hay seemed to fade as tension tightened Vince's chest. He gave a resigned nod, his mind racing with possibilities as he moved his truck and followed the deputy, the weight of the unknown pressing heavily on his shoulders.

Not wanting to cause a scene, Vince moved his truck to the back of the parking lot, the tires grinding over the surface, a background static that joined with a buzzing from a fly. Both annoying, but he ignored them as he found a spot to keep the truck parked. The sun beat down, casting a harsh glare off the truck's metal surfaces, and the air was thick with the scent of hay and the distant aroma of grilled meat from a nearby steakhouse. He locked up truck, the sound of the door latch clicking echoing in the stillness that seemed to have surrounded him.

As he approached the deputy's car, the deputy stepped forward and opened the passenger side door of the front seat. Vince hesitated for a moment, his eyes scanning the interior of the vehicle. No handcuffs, front seat ride. Must be important, he thought, the realization settling in with a mix of curiosity and apprehension.

The deputy's expression was inscrutable, his eyes shaded by the brim of his hat. When Vince asked what this was about, the deputy only shook his head, his lips pressed into a thin line. "You'll soon know," he said, his voice carrying a note of finality that brooked no argument.

Vince slid into the passenger seat, the vinyl hot from the sun and the faint smell of leather and sweat filling the air. The door closed with a solid thud, and the deputy walked around to the driver's side, the sound of his boots crunching on the gravel punctuating the silence. Vince glanced around the car, noting the radio crackling with static and the clipboard with various notes and forms clipped to the dash.

As the deputy started the engine, the car rumbled to life, and they pulled out of the parking lot. Vince's mind raced with possibilities, the uncertainty gnawing at him. The landscape outside blurred past, the familiar sights of the small-town blurring into memories and present. The sights and landscape hadn't changed, with the horizon still giving way to distant sentinel mountains. The air conditioning hummed softly, offering a stark contrast to the oppressive heat outside.

The drive was filled with an uneasy silence, the tension in the car palpable. Vince's thoughts kept returning to the man with the bandage and the look of terror in his eyes. Something big was happening, and whatever it was, Vince had a sinking feeling that it was only the beginning.

As the deputy turned into the parking lot of the local hospital, Vince felt a knot develop in his gut, tightening with every passing second. The hospital loomed ahead, its sterile white walls bathed in the harsh afternoon sun. The familiar scent of antiseptic and fresh-cut grass from the hospital lawn mingled in the air. Vince looked over at the deputy when he stopped at the back door of the building, a heavy silence filling the car.

"Come with me," was all the deputy said, his voice firm yet tinged with empathy. Inside, they walked down the hall toward a double set of doors. The fluorescent lights flickered overhead, casting a cold, clinical glow on the tiled floors. The faint, distant beeping of medical equipment echoed through the corridors, a constant reminder of life and death interwoven within the building's walls.

Margie sat outside the doors on a bench, her shoulders shaking as she sobbed into her hands. Her grief was a palpable force, the sound of her anguish filling the hallway. Vince rushed up to her, his heart pounding in his chest.

"Julian?" he asked, his voice a desperate whisper. Margie shook her head, her eyes red and swollen.

It was then Vince saw the sign over the doors: *MORGUE*. The stark, black letters sent a chill down his spine, the finality of the word hitting him like a physical blow. A man in a white coat came through the doors, his face etched with professional detachment but his eyes showing a glimmer of understanding.

"Are you Vince?" When Vince nodded, the man pushed a door open and said, "We need you to identify a corpse, please. We are told you're the closest kin."

Vince walked through the doors as if in a fog, each step feeling heavy and surreal. The air was colder here, with a slight metallic tang that hung in the atmosphere. Before him on a steel table lay a sheet-covered form, the shape of a body outlined beneath the white fabric. The attendant pulled back the sheet from the top of the table, revealing Kate's face.

It was Kate. Vince's knees almost buckled, and he gripped the edge of the table to steady himself. Her black hair was tousled, the strands spread out like a dark halo.

Her diamond earrings, shaped like horseshoes, glinted in the harsh overhead light. Vince had given them to her, a symbol of their shared dreams and love.

"Do you know this woman? We need a positive identification," the man asked, his voice cutting through the haze of Vince's shock.

Vince barely heard him as he stared at her familiar features, every detail etching itself into his mind. He felt his throat tighten and his eyes burn with fresh tears. The scent of antiseptic and the cold steel of the table contrasted sharply with the warm memories of Kate that flooded his mind.

"Kate Moreno. My fiancée," he heard himself say, his voice breaking with grief. The reality of her loss hit him in waves, each one more devastating than the last. The world seemed to narrow to just this moment, this painful truth, and Vince felt the weight of it crush down on him.

Vince stumbled to a straight-back chair in a corner, his legs barely holding him up. He slumped into it, the weight of his grief overwhelming him. He couldn't hold it any longer. Deep, heavy sobs wracked his body, and large tears streamed down his face, cutting tracks through the dust and grime. His hat fell to the floor with a soft thud, and his head dropped into his hands, his shoulders shaking uncontrollably with the force of his sorrow.

Julian came in and walked over to the attendant, his own face lined with worry and sadness. The room was dimly lit, the harsh fluorescent lights casting cold, clinical shadows. The smell of antiseptic filled the air, mingling with the faint, metallic scent of blood.

"They were both raised in an orphanage together. Neither had family. Only each other. Besides being lovers, they were best friends. Can you tell me how she died?" Julian's voice was steady, but the pain was evident in his eyes.

The attendant, a middle-aged woman with a weary expression, looked visibly shaken by Vince's breakdown. Her voice trembled slightly as she responded. "Blunt force trauma. From the looks of it, something like a pipe alongside the head. But before that, she fought for her life. We found skin under her right-hand fingernails. If they catch the creep who did this, we can tie him to this with DNA."

Julian walked over to Vince and stood next to him for a minute or so, his presence a silent offer of support. The room was filled with the sound of Vince's sobs, each one echoing the depth of his pain. The stark reality of Kate's death hung heavily in the air, a palpable grief that seemed to permeate every corner of the room.

"Come on, pard, I'll drive you home," Julian said softly, his voice a gentle murmur in the oppressive silence. He helped Vince to his feet, the effort almost too much for the grieving man. Vince swayed slightly, the room spinning around him as he leaned on Julian for support. They slowly made their way to the door, Vince's steps heavy and reluctant.

As they reached the door, Vince stopped and looked back at the still form on the table. His vision blurred with tears, but he held the image in his mind, a final, painful farewell. The cold reality of the morgue seemed to close in around him, the sterile environment a stark contrast to the warmth and love he had shared with Kate.

Then, with a shuddering breath, he turned and walked out the door. Margie was waiting outside, her face etched with worry and compassion. She immediately wrapped him in a hug, her arms offering the comfort he so desperately needed. The warmth of her embrace and the faint scent of her perfume provided a momentary respite from his overwhelming grief. Vince clung to her, his body shaking with the force of his sobs, the enormity of his loss settling over him like a dark cloud.

Chapter 4

A few days after Vince had moved back into his own house, Julian drove over to check on him. The late afternoon sun cast long shadows across the yard, the light turning golden as it filtered through the trees. The air was thick with the scent of hay and earth, mingled with the faint smell of horses. Julian found Vince sitting in front of his barn, the corrals behind him holding his four horses and a handful of cows. The rhythmic grinding noise of a bayonet being sharpened on a whetstone filled the air, each pass slow and deliberate.

Vince glanced up as Julian's truck rolled to a stop in the yard, then went back to methodically drawing the bayonet across the stone. The metallic scrape echoed in the stillness, a testament to Vince's focused determination. The past week had been a blur of activity for Vince. He had been prowling the little ten-section pasture, a vast expanse of land dotted with mesquite trees and dry grasses. Each day, he came in with a few cows and a bunch of steers, the sun beating down on him as he worked. He would cut the steers off and return them to the pasture, their bellowing protests fading into the distance. The cows he was holding until he had enough to ship to a livestock auction.

While riding every day, Vince had been vigilant, his eyes constantly scanning for any sign of Pat Borrego's men. The only horse tracks in that pasture were his, a fact that both reassured and unsettled him. But there were jeep tracks right up the middle of the pasture going south, a clear sign that someone had been trespassing. Vince decided he would wait on that jeep to come north. Behind him, leaning against the door frame, was a Korean War model M1 rifle, its dark wood stock polished and ready for use.

As Julian walked up, he noticed the change in Vince. His friend's once easygoing demeanor had hardened. Vince stopped sharpening the bayonet and looked up, his eyes narrowing slightly. "What's up, Julian?" Vince asked. Though his tone was congenial, Julian could tell this wasn't the Vince he knew. His eyes had a steely, determined look, and his chin was stuck out slightly, almost in a challenge to anyone who wanted a piece of him.

Julian took a deep breath, the smell of freshly cut hay filling his lungs. "Oh, not much. Just stopped to see how you were. Haven't seen you since..." Julian's voice trailed off, the unspoken words hanging heavily in the air. The memory of Kate's death was still fresh, a raw wound that had yet to heal.

The silence stretched between them, filled with the distant sounds of cattle lowing and the rustling of leaves in the gentle breeze. Vince's grip tightened on the bayonet, his knuckles white. "I'm managing," he finally said, his voice flat. "Got a lot to take care of."

Julian nodded, understanding the unspoken resolve in Vince's words. He knew that his friend was a man on a mission, driven by grief and a desire for justice. "If you need anything, you know where to find me," Julian offered, his voice steady and sincere.

Vince gave a curt nod, the hard look in his eyes softening just a fraction. "Thanks, Julian. I appreciate it."

The two men stood there for a moment longer, the weight of the past week's events hanging heavily between them. As Julian turned to leave, Vince picked up the bayonet again, resuming his slow, methodical sharpening. The grinding noise filled the air once more.

"I know, since the services. I've been busy. But I'm staying out of trouble, for the time being anyway," Vince finished Julian's question for him, his voice tinged with a weary resolve.

Julian produced two cans of beer from a cooler in his truck and sat down next to Vince. The sound of the cans cracking open was sharp in the quiet afternoon. The cool, crisp beer was a welcome contrast to the hot, dusty air. "How many more cows you got to gather?" Julian asked, taking a swig.

"Half or so. They are out there. It's just those steers of Pat's get in the way. It's okay though, I got nothing else to do, so far." Vince took a swallow of the beer, savoring the brief moment of respite. A dust devil danced across the yard, swirling the dry earth into a mini tornado, and threw dust in the open window of Julian's truck, settling on the worn leather seats.

"What you gonna do when you account for them all? You gonna hunt a job?" Julian was trying to get Vince to open up, his concern evident in the way he looked at his friend.

Shaking his head, Vince looked across the yard at nothing in particular. The corrals, the barn, the distant horizon—everything seemed to blur together in the oppressive heat. "Don't know yet, Jay. I'm taking this one day at a time. I got some accounts to square, then we'll see."

Julian's brow furrowed with worry. "I know there needs to be an accounting, a reckoning, but don't do something that the cost would be more than you can pay. Let the law..."

Vince broke in, his voice hardening with anger. "LAW? The only law around here is Pat's law. I aim to amend the laws he has set down. I got nothing to lose.

Nothing to look forward to. So why not? Maybe what I do will make it better for everyone else."

The air between them grew tense, the weight of Vince's words hanging heavily. The sun dipped lower in the sky, casting long shadows across the yard. The scent of dry hay and the faint smell of horses drifted on the breeze, mingling with the earthy aroma of dust. Julian sighed, taking another sip of his beer. He could see the fire in Vince's eyes, the same fire that had driven him through countless battles and hardships.

"Just be careful, Vince. This path you're on... it's a dangerous one," Julian said softly, his voice filled with genuine concern.

Vince nodded, his gaze still fixed on the horizon. "I know, Jay. But I gotta do what I gotta do."

The two men sat in silence for a while, the sounds of the ranch—cattle lowing, the rustling of leaves, the distant chirping of crickets—providing a backdrop to their thoughts. The dusk settled in, painting the sky with hues of orange and purple, as they sat together, united in their silent understanding of the battles yet to come.

Julian crushed his empty beer can under his boot heel, the crumpling metal sharp against the quiet of the yard. "Look, Vince, if we were free of Pat, and didn't have you, we wouldn't have gained a thing. No matter what you do to avenge Kate, it still won't make her come back. Let the law handle it."

"They can handle it. I'm just gonna help them along a bit." Vince stood up and stretched, his joints cracking audibly in the still air. "I'm gonna make another circle this afternoon. You wanna come along?"

"No thanks, but I've got a head of water running on my cotton. I'll need to change it in a couple of hours. Promise me you won't do anything stupid?" Julian pleaded, his voice edged with concern.

"Nothing stupid. Whatever I do from here on in will be intentional." Vince slipped the bayonet into the scabbard on his belt, the blade sliding home with a metallic hiss.

As Julian drove out of the yard, the sound of his truck fading into the distance, Vince pulled the latigo on his saddle snug around the barrel of a good sorrel horse. The smell of leather and horse sweat filled the air as he worked. Then he stuck the M1 into a saddle scabbard and buckled it in place. Speaking to no one but the horse, he said, "That jeep ought to be coming back this way soon. Let's see if we can't catch sight of them." He mounted and reined the sorrel around and through the gate leading into the pasture, the gate creaking on its hinges as it swung closed behind him.

Vince started south on the jeep tracks, the setting sun casting long shadows across the landscape. He was humming a tune made popular by Webb Pierce, "There Stands the Glass," a melancholy melody that echoed in the stillness. It was Kate's favorite. The memory of her brought a pang of sorrow mixed with anger.

The sun was low in the western sky when Vince rode up to the south boundary fence. The air was cooling, and the smell of mesquite and dry grass was strong. He could see someone had cut the wires and then tied them together with a strand of smooth baling wire. The jeep tracks went through the improvised gate. Vince moved his horse over to the shade of a huge mesquite tree, its twisted branches casting dappled shadows on the ground.

Without taking his eyes off the trail, he reached back and unbuckled the M1 carbine and laid it across the fork of his saddle.

In the distance, he could hear a motor humming along as it made its way toward him, the sound growing steadily louder. A smirk crossed Vince's face as he tightened his grip on the rifle. "I got lots of time," he spoke to the sorrel, the horse flicking its ears in response.

A few minutes later, a white jeep with a cab on it rolled up to the fence. Dust billowed around it as it came to a stop. A tall scarecrow of a man unlimbered out of the driver's side and started untying the wires, his movements hurried and nervous. When he was through, he drove into the pasture, parked, and started tying the wires back up. Vince could see packages wrapped in plastic in the back of the jeep, their contents hidden but suspicious.

Pacer finished tying the last wire and started to turn around when a shadow fell across him. He slowly turned to see Vince sitting there on his horse with the carbine pointing right at his belly. The bandage that had been on his face had dropped and dangled by a piece of adhesive tape to his chin. Terror filled his eyes, the realization of who he was facing dawning on him.

Where the bandage had been, there were four deep scabbed-over marks from his eyes to his chin, angry and red against his pale skin. Seeing the marks, Vince started to tremble with rage, his knuckles whitening as he tightened his grip on the rifle and started to squeeze the trigger. But something inside stopped him. The man before him had killed Kate, he knew it in his soul, but he couldn't bring himself to shoot him.

"Unload that jeep, Pacer, NOW!" Vince growled at him, his voice a low, dangerous rumble.

Pacer stumbled to the rear of the jeep and started pulling the packages out and stacking them next to the jeep, his hands shaking.

"What, what you gonna do?" Pacer mumbled, his voice quivering with fear.

"Don't know yet, but I imagine I'll figure out something," Vince grinned in a malicious way, his eyes cold and calculating. The sun dipped below the horizon, casting the world in twilight as Vince watched Pacer with a mix of contempt and grim satisfaction.

Chapter 5

"Did you kill Kate?" Vince hefted the M1 in Pacer's direction, his voice cold and menacing.

Pacer took a step back, his eyes wide with fear. "It was an accident, I promise! I had her by the arm, she clawed me, and I turned her loose. She stumbled and fell into a pile of pipe. I swear, it was an accident!" His voice trembled, each word a desperate plea.

"The hell you say?" Vince's voice was a low growl. "I need to put you away, but I need you for something else first. Which hand were you holding Kate with?"

Pacer's face fell, his mind racing. "My right, I guess. I don't know, I don't remember. I guess it was my right."

"Put it right here on the hood of the jeep, your right hand, put it on the hood," Vince snarled, his eyes blazing with anger.

Pacer, trembling, slowly put his hand on the jeep, the metal cool against his skin. In a flash, Vince had drawn the razor-sharp bayonet and with a swift, brutal motion, chopped off four of Pacer's fingers. Pacer screamed, the sound piercing the still evening air, and fell backward, clutching the bloody stump of his hand with his left hand. Blood spattered on the jeep and the ground, the metallic scent mingling with the dry desert air.

Vince stepped up to him, his expression hard. He quickly wrapped a bandana around Pacer's wrist, using a stick to twist it into a makeshift tourniquet. The fabric soaked through with blood almost immediately, the bright red stark against the dusty landscape.

"Now, get in that jeep and don't ever come around here again. You go tell Pat I want all my possessions returned in 48 hours or I'm coming for him. That includes this grazing lease. When you tell him, you better get out of state because if I see you again, I'll cut off more than your fingers. You tell Pat no more drugs through here. You hear me?" Vince's voice was deadly calm, his eyes fixed on Pacer's.

Pacer stumbled to the driver's door, whimpering all the time. The pain and fear were evident in his every movement. He fumbled with the handle, finally managing to get in the jeep. His face was pale, beads of sweat standing out on his forehead. When he drove off, the tires kicking up gravel and dust, Vince watched him go with a steely gaze.

Vince moved the packages of drugs into a nearby catclaw thicket along the fence, the thorny branches scratching at his arms as he worked. The air was cooling, but the heat of his anger still burned within him. He mounted his horse and rode back home, the ride silent except for the soft clop of hooves on the dry ground and the occasional rustle of night creatures in the brush. It was late when he reached his place, the stars bright overhead in the clear desert sky.

He turned the horse loose in the corral, patting its neck in silent thanks, then walked into the barn. The familiar smells of hay, leather, and animals greeted him. In a corner where a wooden pallet lay, he uncovered a buried footlocker, the metal box cold and heavy. Raising the lid, he revealed his personal armory. A 12-gauge double-barreled sawed-off shotgun lay on top, its barrel gleaming dully in the dim light. Next to it was a 1911 Colt .45 pistol, army issue, the handle worn smooth from use. Under them were two claymore mines and six hand grenades, their surfaces marked with years of service. A bag of shells for the shotgun and ammunition for the pistol and the M1 rifle completed the collection.

Vince emptied the locker and placed everything on a wooden workbench, the surface scarred and stained from years of hard use. All the while, he whistled the Webb Pierce song "There Stands the Glass," the mournful tune echoing in the barn. It was Kate's favorite, and it brought a bittersweet ache to his heart. He began cleaning the weapons, his movements methodical and precise.

When his weapons were cleaned and oiled, Vince took the two claymores out to the gate that led into the pasture. He placed one at each gatepost, turned slightly in, creating a field of fire that, when set off, the two claymores would sweep everything in a hundred-yard area clean—from a mouse to a ten-foot-tall elephant. When he ran the wires from the claymores back to the barn, he sifted dirt over the wires so they wouldn't be seen. At the barn, he wired both of them into a blade switch. When the switch was closed, the claymores would go off. Then, taking his pistol and rifle, he wrapped up in a blanket in the corner of the barn and dozed off.

Just as it got light enough to see, Vince heard a motor coming up the driveway. Shaking off the blanket, he stepped to the door facing the yard. A Ford pickup was idling into the yard. Two men with rifles flanked the truck and were approaching slowly. One turned at the house and went up the steps to the door. Vince took aim and fired one shot with the rifle. The bullet hit the door jamb just above the man's head, splinters flying. With that, the other rifleman started firing at Vince from behind the Ford truck. The driver of the truck kept rolling toward the gate to the pasture, using the truck for cover. The man at the house fired two shots at Vince, then ran for the truck.

Vince realized the blade switch was across the barn at the other side of the door. As he stepped out to cross the space, a round from one of the riflemen hit his left leg, knocking him to the ground. He scrambled to the switch. Just as he got to it, another round hit him in the side. He reached over and closed the switch before he passed out. A deafening roar ensued. The air was filled with shrapnel. The front of the Ford was perforated in a hundred places. Water ran from the radiator, and the engine stalled. The two riflemen on foot were swept away like a giant hand had wiped the yard clean. The driver, Pat Borrego, was thrown back against the seat. The windshield disintegrated in his lap, his face unrecognizable.

When the deputies arrived, they found the two bodies of the shooters rolled up in a ball of bloody rags with meat showing through. Pat Borrego had his face shredded by the shrapnel. When they found Vince, they at first thought he was dead, but when they rolled him over, a wheeze came from him and his eyes fluttered open. He smiled, then closed his eyes.

At the hospital the next day, Julian and Margie sat next to his bed. When he awoke, he turned his head toward them.

"How am I doing? Will I live another week or so?" Vince asked.

Julian smiled and answered, "Yeah, or at least until you buy me a drink of Jim Beam. You lost a lot of blood. Your leg is broken where the bullet went through, but the doc thinks you're gonna make it."

Margie was trying not to cry.

"And Pat and his boys?" Vince asked.

"Pat is dead for sure. They still haven't figured out the two shooters' identities. They were a mess," Julian explained.

"Good. Now I just need Pacer, the judge, and that brand inspector. But it may be a day or so before I get to them. I'm kinda tired right now." Vince closed his eyes and drifted off.

Chapter 6

It was two weeks before Vince was discharged from the hospital. Julian picked him up and drove him back to his ranch. The drive was quiet, the landscape passing by in a blur of dusty browns and muted greens. At the ranch, Vince saw that the mess had been cleaned up, and the livestock had been turned out into the pasture. One corner of Vince's house looked like it had been sanded by a sandblaster—the paint was gone, and the wood was splintered.

Vince stepped out of the truck and took a long look at the damage. "Damn, claymores are nasty, huh?" was all he said, his voice carrying a mix of awe and regret.

Julian nodded, then began to fill him in on the aftermath. "Pat had no family, and his other employees scattered. Pacer was last seen getting his truck loaded with his belongings and driving away. All of Pat's property is in probate, and the judge is the same one who sent you to prison."

Vince nodded thoughtfully, then asked, "How long is that going to take?"

"At least six months. I figure he'll try to drag it out," Julian explained, his voice laced with frustration.

"We can't wait that long. Those steers are going to grub this pasture out. My cows won't have a thing to take them into calving," Vince explained with a grim tone. "Maybe I need to pay that man a visit."

Julian sighed, shaking his head. "Oh hell, here we go again. You're not healed from the last fracas. Besides, what are you going to tell him? He's a judge."

"He's a human man, is all he is, not some sort of god. Besides, his paycheck is dead. I won't do nothing to hurt him. But first, I'll call the state land department. Maybe they can put a little pressure on the good judge." Vince smiled at Julian, a determined glint in his eyes.

As they walked toward the house, the scent of fresh earth and hay mixed with the lingering smell of gunpowder. The ranch felt different, quieter, almost eerie. Inside, the house was tidy but bore the scars of recent chaos. Vince's bed had fresh linens, and the kitchen was stocked with supplies.

Julian clapped Vince on the shoulder. "Take it easy for a while, alright? You've been through enough."

"I will, Jay. But you know me. There's still work to be done," Vince replied, his voice steady.

Julian gave a small nod. "Just don't do anything too reckless."

Vince chuckled softly. "Reckless is my middle name."

Phil Vickers drove into the yard, Vince and Julian were on their way to the house. The smell of diesel and the dust kicked up by Phil's truck filled the air as a quick swirl of wind pushed the sudden arrival's disturbances towards the men. Phil parked and got out, his boots crunching on the gravel.

"What do you want, Phil?" Vince asked, his voice cold. He put his hands behind him, almost like a military attention stance. Except, he was just moving his hand closer to the pistol he had in a lumbar holster.

"I got a court order here for you from Judge Riley." Phil held the paper over his head. "I have no business with you," he pointed at Julian.

"We have a shotgun inside the door," Julain whispered.

"Put it over there. I'll get to it when I'm done here." Vince shifted his weight to his good leg. He glanced at Julian and motioned his head towards the house.

Julian shrugged and interpreted the motion as a dismissal. He walked across the short distance and entered the house, leaving the two men outside. Vince had his sights square on Phil but had to shift a bit as the leg broken in the shootout with Pat Borrego was still in a walking boot and tender. Phil walked over to the house and put the paper on a table on the porch.

"When you get started gathering to ship, just let me know. I'll come inspect them," Phil said with a sneer.

"No, no you won't. I'll call the state office, and they can send someone else. Don't you EVER set foot on this ranch again. We clear on that?" Vince pointed his finger at the inspector, his eyes hard.

"By state law, I can go on any property I want as an inspector. So don't threaten me!" Phil puffed up, making a point of showing his sidearm to Vince.

Vince stepped closer, his voice low and menacing. "You don't want to test me, Phil. Not today. Now get off my land."

Phil hesitated, then backed down, muttering under his breath as he walked to his truck. Vince watched him go, the knot in his gut tightening. As Phil opened the door, he paused again, glancing at the house, where Julian had entered, back to Vince, several times, like he was pondering the consequences of an as-yet taken action.

"That was no threat. Now git!" Vince move his left hand to balance himself, in case he has to draw, his finger flipping of the pistol's safety.

Instead, the inspector slid into his drivers seat, pulled the door closed, started up the truck. Vince relaxed a bit as he could see Phil had diverted his attention to driving and his eyes were off Vince. As the state truck pulled out of the yard, Vince walked over to the porch and retrieved the court order. It simply stated that he could remove the steers that Pat Borrego had turned out. They were to go to Kelly's Feedlot, where a buyer would pay for them. The funds would go to the court, less the gathering fees and the feed bill accumulated while there. The state leases had been returned to Vince.

He knew that the judge had found a way to get his hands on the money from the cattle sale, but Vince only chuckled. He knew he would add enough liens to the sale price that there wouldn't be anything left for the judge, let alone for him to split with Phil.

Five days later, Vince had corralled 600 steers when a brand inspector from Phoenix pulled into the yard. The sun was high, casting a bright light over the dusty landscape, the air filled with the sounds of cattle lowing and the occasional call of a hawk. A shapely blonde in snug Wranglers, a uniform shirt, and a straw cowboy hat stepped out of the truck, holding her inspection book.

"Are you Vince?" she yelled, her voice carrying over the noise of the cattle to a man sitting horseback in the corral.

"That'd be me. Come on in and welcome," Vince waved at her. The scent of earth and livestock mingled with the warm breeze as she walked through the corral, noticing Vince's walking boot on his left leg.

"Looks like up there is the best place to be. That leg keeping you from getting around much?" the inspector smiled up at Vince, a hint of sympathy in her eyes.

"I do alright as long as I'm up here. If you want, I'll put the cattle down an alley for you to look at," Vince offered. The corrals were set up efficiently, and the blonde walked over to the alley, climbing to the top rail with her papers in hand.

"Bring them on, I'm ready," she called, her voice firm and confident.

Forty-five minutes later, Vince was signing the inspection book, and the blonde inspector was pulling his copies out of the book. The sun was beginning to dip, casting long shadows across the yard.

"I can say this: you're much better to deal with than Phil. And better to look at, too," Vince said with a slight grin, the atmosphere lightening.

"Compliments are always appreciated, but it won't get you any special treatment," she smiled at him, a playful glint in her eye. Vince glanced at the name on the inspection book and saw it was Martha Samuels.

"Will you be doing all my inspections from here on in?" he asked, curiosity and hope mingling in his tone.

Martha looked up, her blue eyes meeting his. "If you keep things as orderly as they are today, I don't see why not. Besides, someone needs to keep an eye on you," she replied, her tone teasing yet sincere.

Vince chuckled, the tension of the past weeks easing slightly. "I'll hold you to that, Martha. Thanks for coming out."

"I think so. Phil is about to get the boot. You're not the only one to complain about him. Are you going to have more to do soon?" Martha asked through the open window of her truck.

Smiling at her, Vince said, "I'll make sure of it!"

When he had paid for the inspection, Vince had gotten a lien form from Martha and filled it out. It would accompany the inspection papers to the buyer at Kelly's Feedlot. Vince had kept track of the market value of the steers and had put a lien amount at just under the net sales price the steers would bring.

"When the judge sees that, he will howl!" Vince said to no one in particular.

As Martha got back into her truck, Vince watched her drive away, the dust kicking up in her wake. The yard was quiet again, but the promise of a new ally in Martha

Samuels gave him a glimmer of hope amidst the ongoing struggle.

Later, he loaded five cattle trucks with the steers and sent them on their way. He called Kelly's to let them know the trucks were rolling their way and that he would be there later to collect the lien. The air was filled with the earthy smell of livestock and the sound of hooves shuffling in the dust as the trucks rumbled out of the yard. Things were coming together.

The sun dipped lower in the sky, casting a warm glow over the ranch. Vince stood by the corral, watching the last of the trucks disappear down the road. The promise of payment and the sense of progress lightened his heart. He knew there was still a long road ahead, but for the first time in weeks, he felt a sense of control returning to his life.

Chapter 7

A week later, Phil came charging through the front gate of Vince's yard, kicking up a cloud of dust. He slammed the pickup door as he got out, the metallic clang echoing through the still air. The heat of the day made the horizon shimmer, and the distant sound of cattle lowing added to the tense atmosphere.

"You think you're pretty damn smart, Vince. That lien was way out of line. I want that money back! The judge is howling bloody murder. Where is it?" Phil demanded; his face flushed with anger.

"In the bank, and there were no limitations on how much I can lien. The judge made out the court order. It didn't say anything about a limit. AND I AIN'T GIVING IT BACK!" Vince leaned forward; his eyes boring into Phil's. The air between them seemed to crackle with tension. Phil's hand hovered near his sidearm, but Vince had already slipped his pistol from behind his back and held it ready. Phil was too intent on staring Vince down to notice.

"Well, don't ship any more of those steers till I talk to the judge. He will have to amend that court order."

"Too late. I shipped the last of them yesterday and collected the lien money too. They will mail the court what's left over." Vince smiled a wicked smile, daring Phil to make a move. Phil stomped onto the ground in frustration, pacing in a tight circle, spitting and cursing.

"Alright, smart guy, where are the six packages you took from Pacer? That's evidence for the probate court. Where are they?" Phil changed tactics, his tone becoming more insistent.

"Probate court my butt. You two got it finagled how to turn everything Pat had into cash. He was bad, but you two are worse!" Vince's voice was filled with contempt, his words laced with a challenge.

The sun beat down on the scene, casting harsh shadows and illuminating the raw emotions on their faces. Phil's eyes narrowed, and he took a step closer, his face a mask of fury. "You better watch your mouth, Vince. This isn't over."

Vince stood his ground, the grip on his pistol firm. "Get off my property, Phil. And don't come back unless you want more trouble than you can handle."

"Where are they?" Phil yelled.

"DEA hauled them off. You're gonna have to settle for your share of the cattle sold when you get the ax at the brand department." Vince kept needling Phil, hoping he would make a move. But crooks are basically cowards, and Phil was the king of the group. When he saw Vince had his pistol in hand, he backed away muttering threats. He went to his truck and jerked the door open.

"Don't come back here. Tell your drug-running friends this route is closed. Any trespassers will pay the price, especially you." Vince warned. As the truck left in a cloud of dust, Vince watched with a smile on his face.

He couldn't get Phil to accost him, but maybe he needed to needle the judge too. He would have to work on that.

Vince pulled up in Julian and Margie's yard and rolled to a stop. The sun was just going down in the west. The porch light came on as he climbed the steps.

"Supper is on the table. Come on in. We've been worried about you." Julian slapped Vince on the back as he came through the door. In the kitchen, Margie was putting food on the table.

"Come sit down before it gets cold." Margie waved them into the kitchen. Vince explained everything that had happened while they ate. Julian smiled at most of it but then made a serious face.

"You know what them crooks might do? You got to them for a lot of money. That hurts them worse than bullets!"

"Yep, I even gave Phil a couple of chances to open the ball, but he backed off. I wouldn't mind finishing this fiasco with them somehow." Vince stuffed a piece of meat in his mouth. Reaching into his shirt pocket, he retrieved a folded check. Handing it to Julian, he said, "Divvy this up with everyone who put up money for me. If it don't cover them all, let me know. There's more where that came from."

When Julian unfolded the check, his eyes bugged out like a stomped-on frog. "There will be money left over. What do I do with that?"

"Hold it for me. I might need a stash I can get to in a hurry. Just don't tell anyone you got it." Vince scooped up a forkful of corn and put it in his mouth. "I'm gonna needle the judge next, so watch out. I want these guys to either make a legal mistake or put themselves in front of my gun. They may not have killed Kate, but they put themselves in a position to start the ball rolling. Sending me to prison was one thing, but killing Kate was going too far, accident or otherwise. I'm gonna square accounts one way or another."

Chapter 8

When Vince entered the courthouse, the metal detector buzzed every time he walked through. He emptied his pockets, revealing the culprit: a pocket knife. The security guards confiscated it and let him proceed. He strolled down the hall, his boots echoing off the marble floors, and approached Judge Riley's office. A redhead sat at the receptionist desk, her eyes narrowing as he walked past without a word.

"Hey, you can't just—" she started, but Vince had already closed the door behind him, shutting her out.

Judge Riley sat behind his desk, his expression sour and worn. Unknown to Vince, the judge's wife and children had left him just two days prior. They had discovered his corrupt dealings and his ongoing affair with the redhead. His mood was as dark as the storm clouds gathering outside the courthouse windows. Vince walked up to the desk, planting both hands firmly on it, and leaned in close.

"You wanted to see me?" Vince's voice was low and challenging.

"NO! I don't want to see you, ever! What are you doing here?" the judge grumbled, barely looking up.

"Well, the brand inspector came by—your brand inspector. He said you weren't happy with the liens I put on Pat's cattle. Said I ought to talk to you. But you wrote out the court order with no specifications on the liens. I just did what came natural. Kind of like you would have. Besides, it's not going to matter in a few days, is it? What with the Attorney General investigating you and that partner of yours. Maybe you'll end up with my old cell at the state prison?" Vince's voice dripped with sarcasm and disdain.

The judge's face twisted with fury. He slammed his fist on the desk, making a stack of papers jump. "You have no idea what you're talking about, Vince. You think you can come in here and threaten me? You're playing a dangerous game."

Vince's eyes were cold, unyielding. "I'm not the one playing games, Judge. You've been crooked for too long, and it's finally catching up to you. I'm just here to make sure you know I won't back down. Not now, not ever."

The room was thick with tension, the air almost crackling with the electricity of their confrontation. Outside, the first raindrops of the impending storm began to patter against the windows, a fitting backdrop to the brewing storm inside Judge Riley's office.

The judge turned pale at the mention of the Attorney General. He pushed his chair back from the desk, opened the middle drawer, and took out a short-barreled pistol. He thumbed the hammer back and pointed it at Vince, his hand trembling.

Vince took a half step back. "Okay, go ahead. You can end it for me right now. No more worries from me. But it won't stop the investigation."

The judge's eyes burned with a mix of fury and desperation. Without a word, he turned the pistol on himself, placing the barrel in his mouth. Vince's heart pounded as he watched, unable to move. The judge pulled the trigger, and the office erupted in a deafening blast. The judge's body fell back against the window, now spattered with blood, brain matter, skull fragments, and hair.

Before Vince could react, a blood-curdling scream pierced the air. He spun around to see the redhead standing in the doorway, her eyes wide with horror as she stared at the lifeless body of her lover. Vince quickly guided her to a chair, her body shaking with sobs. The sound of footsteps thundered down the hall, and within moments, security guards burst into the room.

One of them, a burly man with a calm demeanor, carefully approached the judge's body. He checked for a pulse, then gently placed the judge's arm back in his lap. The pistol was still clutched in the judge's fingers, the smell of gunpowder lingering in the air.

The guard looked at Vince, his expression grave. "Looks like he made his choice," he said quietly, surveying the grim scene. The office was a tableau of chaos and tragedy, the storm outside mirroring the turmoil within.

Vince nodded, his face set in a hard line. "Yeah, he did. And now, it's time for the rest of them to face the music."

In just a few minutes, a sheriff's deputy and an ambulance rolled into the parking lot. When asked about a reason the judge would kill himself, Vince simply said the judge hadn't said a word to him.

"Maybe he just felt guilty for sending me to prison," was all Vince said.

An hour later, he was walking across the parking lot to his truck. "Well, that just leaves one," he said to no one in earshot.

Chapter 9

Vince stood at his kitchen sink washing his breakfast dishes when he noticed through the window a state brand inspector's truck pulling up in the yard. He reached towards the windowsill, picked up his venerable .45, and stuffed it behind the waistband of his Wranglers. Then he saw Martha step out of the truck. A smile crossed his face as he poured a cup of coffee and stepped out the front door.

Martha stepped to the foot of the porch steps and smiled up at Vince. Vince held up the cup of coffee and said, "Come on in, I'll fix you breakfast. Or at least have a cup of coffee."

"Can't. I've got two calls," Martha replied, her hand resting on the handrail, her blonde hair cascading down her back. "But I wanted to let you know, Phil was fired two days ago from the brand department. He swore in public he would get even with you. I thought you ought to know."

"I like that," Vince said with a chuckle. "Gonna get even with me. He tampered with evidence, committed perjury, and sent me to prison while helping ruin my life, setting up my fiancée for rape. And he's going to get even? What a fruitcake."

"Just watch your back. There are three warrants out for him from the Attorney General's office. He may have left the country, but you never know. From what I saw, he's unhinged," Martha warned.

She turned to go. "I'll stop by later for lunch if you'll stand the company?"

"You're on!" Vince called after her.

Vince finished his coffee and went back inside. Moments later, he emerged, pulling his greasy felt hat down on his head as he walked toward the barn. His horses usually had their heads over the fence waiting for him to feed them, but this morning, they stood at the back of the corral, looking toward the barn. Vince took note but thought little of it.

As he stepped through the door into the breezeway of the barn, Vince sensed a flicker of movement in the dim light. Instinct kicked in, and he ducked just in time. A 2x4 whistled through the air, narrowly missing his head. The splinters of wood splashed against the wall where the board had impacted, sending a sharp crack echoing through the barn.

Phil, his face twisted in a grimace of rage, hefted the board again, drawing back for a second swing. Vince's hand fumbled at his waistband, trying to extract his pistol. The hammer of the gun snagged in the fabric of his pants, causing Vince to stumble backward. The board crashed against his shoulder, the impact sending a jolt of pain down his arm that felt like fire racing through his veins.

Phil advanced with a menacing growl, the wooden board held high. Vince, gritting his teeth against the pain, rolled out of the way and scrambled across the dusty floor, his boot sliding against the gritty ground. His breath came in ragged gasps as he wrestled with the pistol. The board came down again, this time connecting with a crunch into the side of his head and sending him sprawling.

As Vince hit the ground, his vision blurred, and the barn seemed to spin around him. He barely managed to twist onto his side, catching sight of Phil's deranged expression as he drew back for another swing. The once-innocuous barn had become a battlefield, the old wooden beams and hay bales now mere obstacles in their deadly dance. A bale nearby still held a bale hook. Vince grabbed it and as Phil advanced, he gathered his strength for a lung and surged quickly forward with a swing, the hook biting into flesh through the attacker's pants and into his thigh. With a shriek of pain Phil stumbled back a step but with a crazed yell gained his balance and advanced again.

With a fierce grunt, Vince finally freed the pistol from his waistband. He rolled to his knees, the barn floor rough against his skin. Just as Phil's board swung down for what would be a fatal blow, Vince's .45 roared to life. The thunderous cracks of the gunshots seemed to split the air with each pull of the trigger. The first shot hit Phil's chest with a resounding thud, sending him staggering backward. The second shot caught him in the shoulder, twisting his body awkwardly. The third and fourth rounds were quick and precise, tearing through the air and hitting their mark and burying inside the man's side.

Phil's eyes widened in shock as the impact of the bullets drove him back. The board slipped from his hands, falling to the floor with a dull thud. His mouth opened and closed, but no coherent words came. He staggered a few steps before collapsing, his body sprawled out like a discarded rag doll against the barn floor. Blood stained the dusty wood beneath him, and the air filled with the coppery scent of his demise.

Vince watched with a mix of exhaustion and grim satisfaction. His breaths were heavy, and his heart pounded with the adrenaline still coursing through him. He slowly set the pistol down beside Phil's motionless form, his movements deliberate and weary. He couldn't feel his head, but there was a resounding pressure building against the side where the board had connected. His vision was blurring quickly. He crawled to the nearest wall and, sitting up, leaned back against it, resting his head back against it. He let his heavy eyes close and whispered to the stillness of the barn, "Kate, we got the last one."

The barn was eerily quiet now, save for the distant creaking of the wooden beams and the gentle rustling of the horses outside. Vince's body ached, and the dust of the barn seemed to settle around him like a shroud. Except, he smelled, flowers?

"I know, cowboy. Rest now."

"What?" He tried to speak but more groaned and thought the word. It couldn't be, but he thought he heard Kate whispering ever so softly, then he lost consciousness.

Chapter 10

When Martha arrived three hours later, her face reflected the shock and sorrow of the scene before her. Vince's once-proud barn had become a grim testament to a life lived on the edge. As she approached, the weight of the past few weeks pressed heavily on her, mingling with the somber air of the barn. Five days later, Julian Ralston, his wife Margie, and a dozen friends and neighbors gathered around a bed of flowers, their heads bowed in respect.

At the foot of the bed stood Julian, his hat held respectfully in his hands. At the head of the line, a headstone stood next to Kate Moreno's headstone. Julian's voice broke the silence, a mixture of reverence and sorrow in his tone.

"They had no family we knew of other than each other. Their whole lives, they depended on each other. Vince served his country, loved only one woman, and tried to be a fair, honest neighbor. He fought his battles his way, the only way he knew. His way may not have been in accordance with man's laws, but it was in accordance with his. Now, they rest together. And we won't ever forget them or what they did."

The sun dipped low in the sky, casting long, mournful shadows over the graves. The scent of wildflowers filled the air, mingling with the faint, lingering aroma of gunpowder and horses. The wind rustled through the trees, whispering secrets of old battles and love lost and found. As the group disbanded, Julian stayed a moment longer, his eyes fixed on the headstones. He nodded once, a silent promise to honor their memory, before turning to walk away, leaving Vince and Kate to rest together in peace.